Compton Reade

Basilissa

the free of a secret craft

Compton Reade

Basilissa
the free of a secret craft

ISBN/EAN: 9783337374433

Printed in Europe, USA, Canada, Australia, Japan

Cover: Foto ©Andreas Hilbeck / pixelio.de

More available books at **www.hansebooks.com**

Basilissa; The Tree of a Secret Craft.

A POEM.

By Compton Reade.

OXFORD:
T. & G. SHRIMPTON, BROAD STREET;
LONDON:
WHITTAKER & CO.

PRELUDE.

HERITRESS sole of beauty was young Basilissa the artiste,
    Born in a cyclone, and lulled to rest by the dirge of the storm-bird,
    Cradled on floods, and baptis'd in the parting sun-tears of sorrow,
Sign'd with a very cross—prophetic emblem of hardship !
Nam'd Basilissa—for why ? her foreground belied her horizon—
Queenly in feature, in shape, though not in purse or in status—
Queenly in voice and in ear, not less than in musical conscience—
Queenly in depth of thought, in poetical vigour of diction—
Queenly in height, in motion, and more than queenly in genius.

  Was she plebeian in pocket, plebeian in plainness of vesture,
Low in her scant of food, in long trapesing walks through the city,
Low in her solitude, her absence of every relation,

A waif, a stray in the fold, the clustering sheep-fold of mortals,

Much too lovely for women to love, too lovely for safety ?

The more angelic the face, the fiercer allurements to ruin.

Hard by the homes of the rich, in lov'd and courted retirement,

Friendless she dwelt with naught else but her Art and her God to assist her ;

Her God, the orphan's God, the friend of the nobly reliant :

Her Art, the language of sound, the inter-communion of nations :

Both she adored as true, unconscious of any distinction,

For to her, God was Art—Art, God existent in music.

Still, though dowerless born, and her Art by most the despis'd Art,

Richest was she in all, save the one thing needful to Mammon—

Rich in a brain, which combined with the commoner gift of perception,

Fancy, colour, and form, and flux of passionate feeling—

Rich in majestic mien ; a face lovely in force, not in weakness,

Yet with the tenderest look, a look so truthfully noble

That the bad were repell'd, as sham'd by the sight of an angel—

Rich in being uncommon, in some sort higher than woman,

Conscious of power innate, of grandeur of soul and intention.

Raising a phantom-belief that the richest are mostly the poorest.

God is more just to each, than even Religion has taught us.

Mortals born of their sires a plain generation of toilers,

Seem to inherit a gift, acquired by ages of service.

Work is to such a fact, quite as much as eating or sleeping,

Nor is the struggle for life decidedly cross to their nature,

Nor destructive of mind, nor quite corrosive of spirit.

In this material life I envy these children of business

Calm content of routine, their live-long drudgery, ceasing

Never, except to yawn, and wish themselves back at their counter,

Dragging the Mammonite chain in most felicitous serfdom.

Some then are born to rule, and others subordinate to them ;

Each having special gifts in their proper employment are honoured ;

Yet I believe in my heart, that the governing soul is transmitted

Down from father to child, nor is lost in the prime generation,

If not in infancy quench'd by sordid contact with baseness.

Not that I claim for the great an inherent virtue of greatness

Either of matter or mind ; t'is only that bearing the daily,

Dull yoke of labour, to such is a galling measure of hardship,

Worse to endure than loss, or the mundane afflictions of most men.

Hence, a dislike of restraint, as the eagle imprison'd in iron

Bursteth the bars of her cage, or pines away in a summer,

Renders the exile of fate perforce a hero—or nothing.

Better not run in the race than slip, and caducous be trampled.

Better not start at the first, than come in with the ruck at the ending.

How can a lady be poor ? There's an equal allotment in all things.

One from the dust is raised, another set down in the mire.

One swallows more than his share of the common provender, whilst a

Lazarus starves for lack of the surplus the glutton consumeth.

Wealth is gotten of need, as the hills encompass the valleys.

Chance sways the course of events, as children a ricketty see-saw.

Nought can endure against Time ; e'en the sons of the Cæsar's are bandits ;

Royalty begs for a mite of his own superscription and image.

Hard is the fate when youth, which should lean on a motherly bosom,

Find, not seek for, advice ; be guided by loving experience,

Know, save duty, no toil, no cares but home and religion,

Forc'd is to fly to One, for strength, for refuge, for counsel,

One to aid her to pay the demand of some Israelite grasper,

One to provide her with bread, with decent raiment to clothe her,

One to instruct her in faith, to retain her brain in obedience,

One to prevent a love from betraying her soul to its ruin,

(Love-excision to one in love is miracle-working !)

While that One is herself, and the head does but feed on the heart-strings.

CANTO I.

AYS which the ugliest prove are not always the darkest in aspect ;
     Thus it fell out, that the sun shone bright to the leaflets responsive,
Windows were deck'd with bloom, the halcyon bloom of the spring-time,
Youth was enjoying its youth, and beauty rejoicing in beauty,
Pleasure was all abroad ; while mirth o'er the visage of sorrow
Carelessly threw its veil—that veil of gossamer texture.
Clouds were dispersed afar ; no future existed but present ;
When at the door of her home came wantonly knocking a lover ;
One of whimsical mien, a sensual free-lance of free-love.

Proud of illustrious birth was Amaranth, son of a Marquis,
Perfect in dress, in style, as noble in gentle demeanour ;

Pre-adamite in descent ; a gold piece every minute,

Safe as the tick of a clock, by year, by month, and by decade,

Dropp'd as it were from the clouds to his sire, a surfeit of money.

Oh ! for one week, one day, of such like celestial fortune !

Lady Belinda, his love, being passing ambitious of music,

Warbling of tune had required, inaudible, aristocratic ;

Splashings of finger too, a touch both graceful and brilliant ;

Somewhat to cover defect, an ignorant effort to polish ;

Not to be learnt in a day, by those engifted with genius,

Nor by the common-place herd can Art be acquir'd in a life-time ;

So must she counterfeit truth ; tell a lie by the aid of a mistress ;

Strive to impose on her peers ; with which benignant intention

Deign'd she to seek as a guide Basilissa, the orphan, and artiste.

Though in this scion both time and tune were deficient, or dormant,

Gushing and soft was her heart, of sympathy keenly susceptive ;

Soon to her joy she found in her fair instructress a jewel,

Priceless, flawless, uncut, yet withal of glistering water,

Strange, prismatic, possessing a charm talismanic in essence.

Hence, this musician she courted,—yes, courted with humble endeavour ;

Pray'd her forget, of rank the purely fictitious distinctions ;

Vow'd her own self the second, and prior asserted the other ;

Offer'd her heart for heart, and clung to her close in affection ;

Gave her the fruit of her lips, the tasteless kiss of a sister ;

Till by simplicity sham'd, and wearied by constant entreaty,

Grace against pride prevail'd ; Basilissa yielded her friendship.

One morn came it to pass as the lady was struggling with nature,

Who, though it made her grandee, had omitted to make her a singer,

Enter, unasked, unobserved, as a listener, Amaranth—loit'ring.

Cold blood from ears to teeth ran across, and then up to his eye-balls,

As issued forth untune from the lips of Belinda the raucous ;

Sudden she ceas'd—and a voice seraphic in metal and brilliance,

Bright as the nightingale's trill, and warm as harps on the waters,

Briefly recited the strain ; too brief—yet enough for entrancement.

Song is the woer of souls, far more than glances, or blushes.

Memory treasures up notes, when the lines of the face are forgotten.

Then he felt in himself that there's something more grand than assertion,

C

Back'd though it be by coin, and the clack of vulgarian toadies.

Which was the typical girl he knew, and' sigh'd for the knowledge ;

Delicate outlin'd the one, as pure mediæval Madonna,

Classical nevertheless, in strength, magnifical, wondrous ;

Voice accordant with shape, and both harmonious in nature,

Show'd forth the woman of women.   While she—she was only domestic !

She, who was holding his pledge on her fine-drawn, taper-like finger,

Malgré her style and air, was a work of commoner moulding.

Many a beautiful hour had Amaranth bask'd in the sunshine,

Toying with sense and shame, and paying a guerdon for kisses ;

Much time too had he forc'd in devotion to Lady Belinda,

Chosen child by his sire, and much belov'd by his mother.

Duty required him to yield his desires to parental affection .

Do not the old know best what really is good for their children ?

Do not the young ones prefer to keep on fair terms with their elders ?

Truest was he of the true to propose to their charming Belinda.

He was the best of boys—for his naughty deeds were a secret.

Craven in soul, but sly, was Amaranth, son of a Marquis.

Therefore, devoid of worth was this tinsel spoilt-child of fortune,

Drunk with an aureole draught, apolaustic, placidly wicked ;

Yet, though foul at the core, the evillest men have their feelings,

Latent perhaps, or stor'd—till some mighty whirlwind arising,

Breaks down the granary doors, a treasure within them revealing.

  Not realis'd are the clouds and snows, and all things supernal,

Down in the valley below ; till you climb the side of the mountain,

Breathing a rarified air, and beholding wonders of colour,

Wonder of size and light, and Alpine shadows, and cities

Lying like dots beneath, and lakes that are smaller than rivers ;

All things are new for the nonce, the past but a vision in distance ;

Low is the old, exalted the new, heaven scarcely is higher.

Thus too reaches the height, the intense, mad apex of pleasure,

Swifter than wings of a dove, than the soaring pinions of eagles ;

Or, than its place in the sky, its bursting place in the night-sky,

Mimic of falling stars, in a luminous shower, the rocket ;

Or, than the fluid electric ; the dazzling flash from the eastward,

Death-bearing, heart-searching, breath-catching, hell-seeking, glorious lightning ;

Or, than conviction, of thought by far the most rapid to travel ;

Love—in the nature of man when first engrafted by music !

Long ere the last modulation had died from the lips of the songstress,

That soft dulcisonant queen, most honour'd by men in the wond'ring,

Amaranth lov'd Basilissa ; and loving, first learnt too, what love means ;

Tremulous rushing of blood—while his eyes beam'd wild with excitement ;

Throbbing of breast to the heart ; his self all lost in emotion,

Stupified, daz'd, and mute, with an indescribable longing,

Gaz'd he, till rose a flush on the forehead of her whom he long'd for ;

Gaz'd he, till rose a frown on the face of the Lady Belinda.

Love at first sound, at first sight, can neither be written, nor painted,

Save as the meeting of twain, who for years have been seeking each other.

Gently the great Lady chid her affianc'd's unwelcome intrusion,

Bade him at once retire, and leave her to finish her lesson ;

Mesmeriz'd as to his eye, it responded to fair Basilissa ;

While distrait with his tongue to his Lady he murmur'd obedience.

Craven in soul, but sly, was Amaranth, son of a Marquis.

Lady Belinda had reck'd of his look at her friend Basilissa,

And like the steel to the soul, quick entered jealousy—demon ;

Not recollecting her vows, her honour, her nobler intention,

Losing her lady-like self in a moment of feminine weakness,

Utter'd she cutting words so cool as to savour of insult,

Seeking a paltry revenge in crushing the artiste—her servant.

　Thus in an evil hour came Amaranth, source of disunion.

Bonds of harmonious love, unresolvable discord dissevers.

　Heard Basilissa—then bow'd—then left in the meekness of silence ;

War in her heart ne'ertheless—the weaker had wounded the stronger.

The, one, friend of her life, unfaithful had prov'd to her promise.

She did not think to be weigh'd with the mere furtive glance of a lover ;

Innocent quite as yet of the priceless price of the keeping,

Aye, the whole of the man, to the girl who is bent on an husband.

So was she angry, indignant, unconscious that she was the traitress,

She whose loveliness turn'd the man from the woman who lov'd him.

Instinct is oft-times true, though unjust to outward appearance !

Coolness however in place of love makes a woman rebellious.

Temperless beauty is rare—Basilissa when wroth was relentless.

" Fool ! from diverging lines to imagine a parallel lasting !

" She to her Art was bound, this other was destin'd for honour :

"Life and aim to each were apart, incompatible, distant :

"Neither were equal in brain, nor either equal in fortune :

"One the owner of rank, the other the pris'ner of talent :

"How she despised the success of adventitious advantage !

"Few words express a thought, but the strangest misnomer is friendship!"

Thus they parted, and thus to her door came Amaranth knocking,

One of whimsical mien, a sensual free-lance of free-love.

Radiant then was the morn, illuminate fierce by the sun's rays.

Sun that shines on the good and the evil, the just and the unjust ;

Sun that the sufferer mocks till he cries, "would God it were evening !"

Sun that rises on shame, on murder, suicide, blood-stains ;

Sun on the nodding hearse, on the garnish'd bridal coruscant ;

Sun on the gaol, on the crank, on the very gallows ridescent ;

Meaningless, double-faced, false, yet ever-jubilant sunshine !

Amaranth walk'd like the sun, the sun in a firmament cloudless,

Sparkling, brilliant, and bright, and always remarkably genial—

Light, and dispenser of light—gold, and dispenser of gilding—

Warm, and dispenser of warmth—gay, and dispenser of laughter—

Liar, dispenser of lies—fool, and dispenser of folly.

Open the door! let him in! be courteous, for courtesy's costless!
Measure your strength against his, your simple trust, with his cunning!
Try if your heart is stone, your pride sufficient protectress!
Cherish an asp in your breast! It bites not—fond Basilissa!

"Came he as patron of Art, a brother to seek for a sister,
"Genius adoring; he hop'd, he should not be deem'd an intruder—
"Her talent was not unknown, he simply desir'd to befriend her."
Yet was his tongue belied by an eye remorselessly hungry,
Peeping from under a lid half-clos'd to disguise its intention.

Fascinates as with a stare the tiger a shivering lambkin,
So was his game to play with, embrace, and fondle his victim.
"Love," he call'd her as yet, for most euphemistic is Satan,
And, as an angel of light, is glorified most in his triumphs.
That cruel eye did its work, a fertile brain help'd the features,
All mock-modest to cheat, (as of old did Judas, the traitor,)
Cheat the girl of her heart, almost of her soul and her reason,
Cheat with a kiss of peace—a kiss emblematic of night-shade.
Never before had she met a thing so transparently varnish'd,

Perfect in all its lines, ingrain'd by careful veneering.
Better than real is sham, till you rub off the surface of shamness.

Courtly in little things, (little things are dearest to women,
Judging a man by his gloves, or the studied droop of the shoulders,)
Amaranth knew how to please ; what time to sympathy simper,
What time in delicate vein imperceptible flattery flatter,
Praises of dress, or of style ; sneers at contrary modes of adornment ;
Coinciding, enquiring, forswearing, admiring, and hinting
Much abasement of self : the most exalted enthronement
Far beyond titles or mode, of her, Basilissa the peerless.
Next he elected to scorn his possible bride of compulsion,
Lady Belinda, the plain, the chos'n of his father and mother ;
Union is forced on earth, but marriage is joined in heaven.
She might become his spouse—his life, his happiness, never !
High, too high was his soul to care for an insolent nothing !
One so untrue to a friend, would be doubly false to a husband.
Thus, he woed her with skill ; and she, unsuspecting and faithful,
Play'd with the artifice laid, as a bird with the snare of the fowler.
Practice had taught him this fact—that a fair one will banish a lover,

Earnest, honest, and true, and above-board in every dealing,

When, she will yield up her soul to an actor's cajollery, helpless—

Therefore the worse the intent, the better the chance of succeeding !

Hypocrite, reprobate, sly, was Amaranth, son of a Marquis.

Drank Basilissa his words, as a camel a stream of oasis.

Instinct, for long had crav'd for some such nectareous flowings,

Vanity's thirst to assuage, or else to intoxicate fancy.

Traitress she half-felt to Art, because She is so universal,

When she beheld at her feet prostrate a minion of Mammon.

Still though her smiles told a tale of his very prosperous pleading,

While her eyes grand in their size, their colour, intensity, meaning,

Spake what her lips utter'd not, with mightier eloquence, still she

Modest retirement display'd, and her tongue and her face were at issue.

Honey is sweet to the soul, but a queen-bee may not confess it !

Somewhat discourag'd, he paus'd, for through tact a repulse is precluded,

Practis'd in easier love, by reserve of maidenhood puzzled,

Till he detected her cheek rubescent with blushes of pleasure.

Then a respectful adieu, as a sycophant pays to an empress,

Dubious pressure of hers, by his waxen, delicate fingers,

D

Lady-like, tapering, soft, in one word—aristocratic—

" Might he presume so far as to trespass upon her to-morrow ?

" He had an offering to bring, a rose, and milk stephanotis,

" Orchids exceeding rare, only rear'd by the Amaranth hot-beds.

" No?   Then surely, by heav'n was his silly temerity punish'd ;

" He should have sigh'd from afar, till heard were his wishes in dream-land,

" Present with her in the night, that she might in the dawn of some morning,

" Recognize him as the one who was fated her friend sempiternal!"

Laughing, she answered his flam with the ringing, numberless laughter,

Emerald wavelets resound on the lake-like shores of the Solent.

  Then, having *left its sting*, the wriggling, mèrciless wasp-form,

Flutter'd away to vice, being somewhat of purity wearied ;

Essence of life to this man, and its one necessity—pleasure ;

Sin, the desire of his soul, his cherish'd and constant companion.

Left her his sting as a gift ! as a mad dog leaves hydrophobia !

Scorpions poison of blood, or the gad-fly maniacal longings !

  Babylon—City of men—Thou manifold mart of the nations !

Babylon, Christian, Christless, commingling of angel and demon !

Babylon, joyful in gin, and drunk with the labourer's wages !

Teeming with streets and squares, the highways and bye-ways of feasting,

Teeming with alleys and courts, the low ways and dank ways of starving,

None of thy millions of souls, with their million unclassified sorrows,

Grinding some to the bone, to the brain, to the still Stygian river,

Merit my pity so much as entrapp'd Basilissa the orphan.

When on the ocean of life our bark bursts away to the sun-ward,

Borne by some favouring blast, and counter to earth's revolution,

So that it follows the light in its course as the needle the magnet,

Whirlpools afar appear—rocks, deep in the clarified waters

Sunk, unremember'd are past, and our sails in perpetual noonday,

Strain to the buoyant breeze, nor reck of a possible storm-wind,

Bounding expectant along to some fatuous goal in the distance,

Thinking to travel as fast as the trail of the monarch of heaven.

Love is the pilotless bark that bears to —— it matters not whither,

Heav'n or Hell upon Earth, remorse, or exquisite rapture,

Or, to the idol self, be-ruddled with paint egotistic,

Dagon of this our age, and doom'd, like Philistia's Dagon,

Sooner or later to fall to the ground from its pedestal lofty.

Thoughtless of all but one thought, insensate of aught but one feeling,

Musicless save of one strain, dreamless of all but one dreaming,

Phantasied, mesmeriz'd, bound by a spell was poor Basilissa.

Memory brought back his face, his glances, his smiles and his accents,

Wrong preference for herself, yet righteous scorn of Belinda.

Charms of the snake by the charms of a song allur'd to her bosom.

Oft repeated again was the whole, and again till the ev'ning,

Fifty times told was that tale in caprice, nocturne, and sonata ;

Then, in the dreams of the night, revers'd with the strangest additions ;

Then, in the grey of Aurora, a grey that melts into golden ;

Last, in the ring of a bell—a tap—and Amaranth entered.

Clasping of hands, and weaving of arms, and tangle of chesnut

Locks, with light auburn curls, all twin'd with a cincture of scarlet ;

Soft as the ripples of brooks, were their gentle murmurs susurrant ;

Eye was wedded to eye, cheek to cheek, and dimple to dimple ;

Sparkled the torch of love, till it burned with exquisite fury ;

Little they cared for speech, lock'd fast in nervous embraces ;

He with his satiate soul, by her warmth, as warm'd as astonish'd ;

She with a novel delight inebriate, revell'd indulgent.

Not one thought did she give to the feelings of Lady Belinda,

(Quondam the friend of friends,) who writh'd from the sore of desertion,

Which is the blinder in love, love or self, self knows not, love cares not.

As on the softer sand, the spring-tide shaping its wave-shapes,

Fashions a mimic storm, the trough, the sweep and the crest-foam :

So ere the tide receded of passion the imprints procellous,

Scored in billows the soul eternal of mad Basilissa.

Day after day, for long hours flow'd and ebb'd the furious spring-tide,

Leaving a higher mark each time of its lashing the sea-shore.

Week after week, with his flowers, his gifts, his smiles, and caresses,

Hungry-hearted yet wary, expectant, watching, and hopeful,

Amaranth sought the home of the girl he lov'd falsely, but fiercely.

One morn, he came not, and she—she was lacrymal, agonis'd, angry.

One morn, he came not, for he had a scene with his father, the Marquis.

Lady Belinda the spurn'd, forgotten, neglected, forsaken,

Followed her swain, through a spy, to the door where dwelt Basilissa,

Fact reveal'd to her facts ; and in fury at falsehood of friendship,

Curs'd she the felon who snar'd her own pet lamb from its sheep pen ;

Curs'd she the traitorous slave purloining her patron's affianc'd.

Mortified then, but in terror of loss, she appeal'd to the Marquis ;

Urg'd him to save his son from the claws of a wily intriguante,

Hoping thereby to regain her recreant, kneeling for pardon ;

Better to keep him by force, than to yield to the fraud of a rival.

Threaten'd with loss of lands, of prospects, of honour, of future,

Tired perhaps of a game with unassailable virtue;

Craven in heart, though so sly, the prodigal shew'd the white feather,

Vow'd he was sick of the husks of a swine-fed, vulgarian beauty ;

Came to himself—that is—to his greedier, Mammonite, base-self ;

Feasted on fatted calf, and bow'd in the humblest submission ;

Grovell'd before his betroth'd, who was graciously pleas'd to be lenient ;

Quite surrender'd his Self, his love, his life, to ambition ;

Or to a cowardly dread of some unpronounceable evil ;

Cast forth the pearls from his breast, and incontinent crush'd them to powder.

" He might be ill," Basilissa opin'd, but would not enquire.

She to betray her own, her darling own by impatience !

Guess'd she the bathos of pride, the frivolous pride of a Marquis.

Surely a lady-like mind is better than coronet's blazon !

Old-blood, she flatter'd herself is equal to parvenu titles.

Higher than all is Art, the giv'n inspiration of heav'n.

Those, who would follow that guide, must be meet for her whom they follow ;

Like her in some sort, and so, not courting but courted for Art's sake.

" He might be ill—He would come—How strange that he wrote not a letter !"

Neither missive, nor clue to the shameless track of the robber !

Torn was the fire from her heart : her veins were congealing to ice-balls.

Heartless inept to toy with celestial, passionate yearnings !

Heartless to play with a soul as a child with a favourite spaniel !

Hope against hope, until all the heaving bosom was sicken'd.

Hope against hope, until love was all but converted to hatred.

Hope against hope, till her glory had sunk to the veriest Tophet.

Hope against hope, till to hell was her foolish Paradise changed.

Ah me !—who knows, who knows, the heft of a self that is weighted !

Patience a sign is of truth ; faith against appearance is faithful ;

Constancy proves a whole-heart, but who can endure disappointment?

Wearisome, irritant, long, that bids fair to be everlasting !

One whole month did she wait believing against her conviction ;

One whole month suffic'd as a test-time to prove him ; but after

Dim in the twilight she prick'd a meandering vein in her bosom ;

Free-flowing, straight from her heart, incarnadine, roll'd forth the ichor,

Staining her boddice of white, and the flesh transparently whiter.

Next, by the glow of the moon, intermingling tears with the carmine,

Words, burning words from the soul, the paralysed soul by his wronging,

Flow'd on a music sheet ; writ line by line with the virgin-

-Sanguen hallow'd by grief; she charg'd him his verdict to utter,

Once and for all ; for ever and aye ; for now, and for certain ;

Sharp, decisive, and clear, as the judge on the prisoner's carcase ;

Either to make her his bride, and to lead her to pleasures Elysian,

Greenness of widening sward ; streams cooling a summer eternal,

Trees of perpetual shade, and flow'rets gay without number,

Lays of the linnet and thrush, or of nightingale—nature's orchestra ;

Goblets of luscious wine, and the magic, fantastical colour,

All-empurpling in tint the distance, the scene, and the fore-ground ;

Mystical trance of love, that trance of exquisite feeling,

Centuries spending in hours, a myriad lives in a life time ;

Naught existing to each, save each, and either to other.

That—yes—that, or to die—the speedier parting the better ;

Lethe the cup of the slave, the soothing cup of the soul-sore ;

Lethe whose baptism laves the hopeless in sweetest oblivion !

Farewell to Art with a sigh—Art true—Art constant and faithful !

Art never fades, nor fails ; she sings as of old to her fautors,

Sings with a tongue unknown, to the world of ignorant scoffers !

Farewell to Love the false, as the dove escap'd from her prison,

Surplic'd in wings, and swift, is free, though for ever unquiet ;

Lost to her mate, her all, she chants one mournful cadenza ;

Then lies her down to sleep, the death of unsatisfied longing !

    Thus, in fanciful mood, but with fell suicidal intention,

Swore by her blood to die, by her blood swore, mad Basilissa.

    Sore distress'd was the man, the man who was wright of this soul-work ;

Fearing delirious act, from the ghastly hue of her letter,

E

Scribbled in rubric type; but not the red of the printer;

Rhetoric, wild from below, and conscience-convicting as Judgment.

As from the confluence strange his bad eye could not be averted,

Ran through the dirt of his breast a current stirr'd up by pity.

Fear'd he a father much—blood-guiltiness more than a father.

Promptness in deed was required ; too late a day, or an hour !

Still he was tied by the hand—her door was watch'd by suspicion ;

Spies were around his path, he was chain'd by the fastest of fetters.

Visit her ! Ah ! what else could arrest the suicide's mania !

No ! the risk was too great—by a lie he might reassure her—

Doubtless his cue was to lie; no novice was he in the black art ;

Falseness his mother's milk—cajolery taught from his cradle,

Lying was part of himself, an article quite of his credence.

After a turn of the brain resolv'd he to temporise deftly ;

Time is a healer of all ; she would live down the strength of her passion ;

Wisdom equivocates well to save the heart wrung to madness;

Specious wisdom will stoop to deceive with prospects ideal.

He knew the blind side of her; he could laugh in his cheek on the blind side,

Whispering fallacy, froth, and offering shadow for substance.

Safe by a trusty hand he sent her the following letter.

"My Basilissa, my own, thou choice of a heartfelt devotion,

"Doubt me not—do not despair ; my love is the same now as ever !

"Deeper in absence, 'tis true ! would God 'twere more shallow by presence !

"For I am pining for love, a compulsory prisoner from thee !

"Yet in this world we must be of the world, though less worldly than world-like,

"I cannot sink my estate, my rank, my honour, my status.

"Over-bespatter'd with mud of disdain, to my equals degraded,

"Thus to confront me, I swear, is the furthest thought from your forehead !

"Nor dare I, even by deed of right, to inherit the curse of

"One, who his father's grey hairs to the grave brings downward in anguish.

"Bigoted, stern, is the Marquis—and I—I am thrall'd to obedience !

"Yet am I pining for love, a compulsory prisoner from thee.

"You would be Amaranth's bride, would stand before men as his mate-dove—

"Ah ! could it be so now, to-day, at once, and for ever !

"Not as a bar should you be, 'twixt a son, and his wrong-headed parents,

"Nor as an interloper be held, nor be snubb'd by the women

"Pointing the finger of scorn, twice over, through jealousy ; these are

"Some of the pitfalls that lie in the way of a proximate union.

"Amaranth puissant is born ; and you—you are puissante by culture,

"Yours is the gentle blood ; his—fortunate, noble, illustrious,

"Richer to-day with mankind than Shakespeare, Raphael, Handel.

"You to the Pharisees crass, you are naught but a penniless teacher !

"Much as a nurse instructs a child how to eat like a Christian,

"So do you train in scales, in minims, and crotchets, and quavers,

"Simply a framer of sound—so far are our fortunes unequal.

"All that is nothing to me—*quoad* me— for in lady's demeanour,

"Aye, and in lofty brow, in star-like firmness of future,

"Aye, and in spirit to rule, in all the grandeur of true love,

"You stand alone—by yourself—a peeress—a princess potential,

"Regnante in clouds of mind, enclos'd in a halo of genius.

"Still in this cold, mundane, ridiculous, kosmical fact-life.

"Gold is gold, and rank is rank, and talent a bubble,

"That may soar up into air, or else like the quicksilver, rolling

"Mayhap adhere ; mayhap, be scattered to numberless atoms.

"Therefore say I to my love, if my love would mate with her lov'd one,

" Not being born of luck, of Mammon, coronet, vapour,

" Only of Art, of life, of loveliness, sentiment, feeling,

" Make you your own fame so bright that all women shall worship its reflex ;

" Just as the African fools bow the knee to the sun that is rising,

" Be it, the God they adore is equally godlike in shadow.

" Hang not your head in gloom, and droop not in sordid retirement !

" Blaze forth your hue to the crowd as the red azalia in summer.

" Being uncommon, surprise the open-mouth'd multitude, gaping

" Moon-struck at every trick of the newest miracle-worker.

" Thus shall you rise to my height ; yes, darling ! equal to equal !

" Parity ; that can alone put a stop to the caviller's cavil.

" You shall be more than wife—to affectionate parents a daughter,

" Strain'd to a motherly breast, no longer the orphan forsaken.

" In every grade is the meed of successful adventure—affection.

" Then, Basilissa, mine own, be brave, be true to your instincts !

" Doubt me not, never despair of an end to a forc'd separation !

" Be what you are—what your will is to be—the woman of women !"

There was a meaning in this—blind trust had confided ambition,

Presentiment, realising of dreams, a mighty volition.
Weak at the best is confession; but weakest of all—to a courtier !
Smiling he heard her ideas, in their improbability, garish.
Now they would serve his turn; 'twas thus that he falsely cajol'd her,
Hoping for Lethe of love in the vain pursuit of vain-glory.

Art is a solace in woe, a comfort, an aid, and a blessing,
Somewhat rewarding her slave for the life-long toil of the learning;
But the one strength to resist, insane desperation to master,
Victory, triumph o'er self, when self is a selfish tormentor,
Rending the heart to shreds—that alone is the gift of Religion.
Then the Christophilous one finds a Christ, and a friend, simultaneous ;
Christ instead of the cross, a friend as a guerdon of friendship.
Faith, Basilissa had not. The Sadducee stamps on the artiste ;
Nothing would grate on his ears so much as the cantos of angels.
Even the Catholic smiles a languid approval on genius ;
Priests do not like God's-gifts external to be to the priesthood.
Thus, 'twixt Belief and Art will the struggle continue, unequal,
Until the lion of truth to the lamb of beauty be wedded ;

CANTO II.

ISIONS appear in the dark, midst the sombre moments of slumber,

     Not to prophets alone.   They arise before commoner mortals—

Ones of to-day, and to-morrow, of yesterday, ones of the Kosmos—

Reflex, may-be, of events in the stars, yet plain to the sleeper.

Once I have thought that awake, I am here ; asleep, I'm in Venus,

Sirius, Jupiter, Mars, or the belt-revolving of Saturn.

Do not tell me my dreams are mere terrestrial puzzles ;

Shuffles of common facts, knaves, deuces, aces, and trump cards ;

Transposition of lines, and metrical forms of mosaic ;

Falling down actual stairs, with an immaterial bottom ;

Flying an actual foe at a pace more rapid than railroad ;

Stabb'd by a very sword ; as by day, by the fork'd tongue of malice ;

Drowning in real depths, till the floods bubble over your eyelids ;

Sicken'd by gashes and blood, or by jabbering features of idiots ;

Gruesome in soul, as one who has enter'd the portals of Hades,

Hand to hand with the damn'd, or cheek by jowl with the corpses ;

Kissing a putrified being, alive ; nor soulless,—or why this

Quick, inarticulate talk, and moving of tongue as in torment ?

Why to the Crucified cry to remove such company from me ?

Pray for a thousand deaths to gain but one annihilation ?

Hell is to me but a law of association with evil ;

And in visions I learn the best and the truest of lessons ;

Visions, the emerald life, as the planets in darkness coruscant.

Dreamed a fever'd dream—a dream of sight, and of touching,

Painful, intense, unavoidable, staring all ways like a slain-face,

Parch'd Basilissa in tongue, in lips, in strain of the cheek-skin,

Tossing amorphous sheets with a fitful, hysterical motion.

Words are but colourless modes to paint a picture of star-land,

Whether of luscious sense, or the torment of venient torture,

Thrills, throbs, shaking in fear, lights vivid, shadows opaquest

Outlin'd sharply, as edges of clouds electric in essence.

Words are but colourless—Hence, a dream-tale is merely suggestive.

F

THE DREAM OF THE PARABLE-GARDEN.

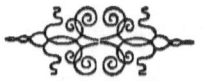

-RED-GAY garden of flowers, all crowded with fairest of girlhood.
  Hot was the sun over-head, around all pulverine, thirsty ;
Though the bloom was so scorching, all gaudily crimson and scarlet,
Not a leaf on the trees but of copper ; nor blade of the green-grass ;
No nor one speck of blue, or gray, to chill the caloric.
Every cheek was flush'd, the eyes were bloodshot, while anger
Brow-pervaded each one, as they cried, but vainly, for water.
Prisoners these of thirst—Their rich apparel, resplendent,
Dusty withal, of silks, and lace, and orient jewels.
Walls this garden enclos'd—walls high as walls of a castle,
Brick-dust red like the flow'rs, like the rubies in beauty's tiara.

One little door at the side—It was lock'd, for all those were captives.
Knew Basilissa, somehow, perhaps with the instincts of star-land,
This was the harem of one, who driv'n by fate from his empire,
Left his own bevy of loves, in his haste to flee from the foemen,
Fasten'd by bars of iron in this arid, midsummerly pleasaunce.

Watch'd she their talkative ways, despair that quarrels from temper,
Spiteful, unreasoning, sly, vindictive, nasty, capricious.
Somehow she was, and was not confin'd with them in their durance ;
Quicker than play-wrights art, oft-times star-scenery changes.
None of them recognis'd her, nor felt she at home with the women,
Ignorant, quite of their names, their habits, thoughts, aspirations.

Anon they mov'd to the door, a small, but impervious, portal,
Weighty as tons of lead, clamp'd across with iron mordacious,
Guarding the fair from aught else, but the love of the lover, who bought them.

First, a Circassian, tall, blue-ey'd, of magnifical whiteness,
Baring a bosom opal, with locks more topaz than amber,
Pouting an osculant lip, cornelian, as sensual morning,
Wrench'd at the door till the force burst a nerve in her marble-like fore-arm,
Moving the grace from her brow, but not the hinge in its socket.

Then a Being of night, warm, luscious, passionate, lust-ey'd,
Supple and springy in shape, irate from the drought and the sun's heat,
Fever'd in temples, as oft in her wilder commerce with men's hearts,
Tried it, and tried it again, till she fainting fell from exhaustion.

All in their turn essay'd, some peevish, some rampant, more wretched.
"What will become," they cried, " of the diamond houris of pleasure ?"
Echo replied "What !" "What !" from the walls surrounding the pleasaunce.

Hotter the sun's-rays burnt, inflaming the throat and the palate,
Mocking their libertine clothes, their gew-gaws, and glories of splendour ;
Gnashing their teeth, with dull hand, they group'd as for safety together.

She, Basilissa, perceiv'd that the exit was adamant, futile,
Nor would she double her thirst, by the toil of a fruitless endeavour,
Yet did she fumble the door, and wondered much at its firmness ;
What could be on the reverse ? a mystery ! rising on tiptoe,
Close she applied her eye to the small *lorgnette* of the grating,
Curious alike, and in hopes of finding release for the captives.
Why does her heart beat hard, as the swinging strokes of a piston ?
Why does her bosom heave, as the breast of tempestuous ocean ?
Why does her breath stop short, uncertain as if of returning ?
'Tis for another scene, she views, but does not take part in !
One containing a unit, small, yet to her universal !

Straining of sight is troublous, and deep agitation is weary,

Yet moves she not from the door, nor her eye from the mystical grating ;

For on the other side, by the coolest fountain of water,

Rippling, showering, sweet, as though to tantalise fever,

All-delicious to taste, to sight, and in murmur æolian,

Amaranth sat as one in despair, hypochondria's victim,

Maz'd in expression of face, and chlorid in hue of complexion,

Dull, down-hearted, as one from a loss unregainable suffering ;

Nigh him Belinda, the girl who held his pledge on her finger,

Bane of his beautiful life, and her own detestable rival,

Toying with him unwilling, and taking, instead of receiving,

Paying herself in embrace, in kissing, fondling, caressing,

Much as the mad of dead-love be-slobbers an idolis'd statue,

Hugging marmoreal ice, as if 'twere the very departed ;

So woed she Amaranth cold : far more irresponsive than marble.

Gaz'd Basilissa a time ; then, joy'd at this test of the cordial,

Heart-whole love of her love, she cried, to make surety the surer,

His name and hers in one ; as though now indissoluble always.

Cried in the pain of joy ; the waterfall laughter, that mimics

Anguish in mortal eyes—proof that joy and grief are relations.

Flash'd at once the dull orb, as the dawn on the snow of the mountains ;
Heav'n seem'd return'd to his brow, a heavenly smile to his features ;
Hastily tracking the voice so dear, he quitted Belinda,
Ran to the door, and breath'd its musical tones through the grating.
Breath'd till her sense seem'd steep'd in a soft, miraculous feeling.

" How, 'dearest,' how to escape, once again to have you, to hold you"
Utter'd, she, wildly, and eager, for precious is every second,
Precious to her who craves for peace for a tremulant bosom.
" Save these who perish of thirst, save me, who am dying of longing !
" Hope for too long deferr'd makes its prisoner sick of deferring.
" Drinking is little to me, my drought is not physical, your lips
" Sensible bear to my sense a springing fountain of gladness."
" Darling !" exclaim'd she again " for love's sake, unfasten this portal."

Gravely he shook his head with a look of intelligence pallid,
Doubting apparently hope, as her wild supplication he answer'd :

" Bars between earth and heav'n, irrefragable hinges of iron,
" Bolts colossal in mould, fraught by sternest social invention,

" One, cannot move, nor two ; the only lever is number.

" Combination is strength, and unity defies units,

" Mostly the motive power—use these thirsty gauds as your items ;

" Each in herself is weak, Circassian, Moorish, or Grecian,

" Yet has the total a weight to which this door is a feather.

" Promise them drink, and they will obey the avatar of water !"

    Then with a half-blown kiss, he slow return'd to Belinda,

Back to the Lady whose love was tiresome, forward, asserting,

Even to wearing away a stone by continual dropping.

    Fast to the circle of girls bemoaning sadly their fortune,

Fainting with heat, but firm, ran back Basilissa, the dreamer.

Fire from her fiery lips broke forth in eloquent language,

Fire that spread to a blaze, scintillatory, enthusiastic,

Breast-igniting and brain, inflammable, fierce, pan-ardescent.

" Lead Basilissa" they cried " Lead on, Thou saviour, we follow."

Soon from the bosom of snow torn off was the scarf and the boddice,

Drapery wrench'd from the limbs, and cincture bright from the waist-band,

Fillet from off the hair, with delicate Indian linen,

Interwoven together in shreds, tight-handled, firm-twisted,

Framing a rope of such sort, as indeed to sight was surprising;

Millecouleur, end to end ; gilt, argent, azure, and ruby,

Emerald, amethyst, vert, opal, violet, purple, and orange.

Patch'd, incrongruous, quaint, impossible sequence of colours.

Nor were the girls unlike a group of bathers undressing,

Finery-stripped, and thus enabled to muscular action,

Clad but in loosen'd white, and lovelier far for the freedom,

Zoneless, lissome in grace, and supple in elegant motion,

More in accordance with ease than the uglier dictates of fashion ;

Too suggestive perhaps for the coarse, the everyday swinish,

Nature was fram'd for Eve, and the purity primal of Eden;

Yet the freer the dress, the nearer the Paradise-model ;

Freedom, is God's-gift to all, and all free things are celestial.

Tight to the adamant door, looking more unyielding than ever,

Through the handle of steel, attach'd to the framework by rivets,

Part of the portal itself, they fixed the coil they had twisted ;

Then with impatience of thirst, demanded the order for action.

Two by two at the rope, arrang'd they take up their station,

Each girl a link in the chain, the well-wrought chain of salvation,

She, Basilissa, their queen, disposing obedient subjects,

Loud exhorting, and firm to be ready, be steady, be urgent,

And at the word to pull one mighty pull altogether.

  Last, erect, at their head she stood, majestic in gesture,

Feeling her will ruling theirs, as the pilot the vessel enormous ;

Proud in superior force she paus'd—then shouted the signal—

Crash fell the door to earth—and crash !—her spirit awaken'd.

  Feverish floods abated—and she read the vision of star-land

Parable-like in its lines by the light of Amaranth's letter.

Thought was the parent of deed ; and the offspring of deed disappointment.

END OF CANTO II.

G

CANTO III.

UTTERINGS low in the squares, in the terraces, Opera, ball-rooms,
   Theatres, concert-halls, Row, in the Parks, the carriage, the boudoir,
Fanciful glance, and signal known, and mystery mystic,
Feminine, yet neither dress, nor gossip, nor folly, nor mischief,
Servitor-worship of wealth, nor gentle adoring of peerage,
Osculant fawning on things whose shell is attractive, though empty ;
No, nor worship of things, that are clever, but butcherlike, cruel,
Sporting most with poor fish, who offer themselves as an off'ring ;
Weak fish gorging a bait, though seeing the hook that is in it ;
Weak fish loving to death the barb that rends them asunder.

Mutterings low by night in bed-room confidence whisper'd,
Much excitation, and much sibillation of musical treble,

Toilet-stories the more, by a spice unaccountable, piquant—

Microcosmical, veil'd, unreveal'd, sensational, problem—

Underbreath, furtive, quaint, the marvel of marvels—the secret—

Curious girlhood athirst for a vain curiosity, simple

Girlhood, that laughs at creeds, but accepts the assertion of bombast,

Unsupported by aught, save the potent logic of large eyes

Looking unutt'rable thoughts, inasmuch as they've no thoughts to utter.

Masonry silent, yet real, is free though in brotherly bondage;

Masonry places a man on a pedestal higher than others.

Craft may be crafty, but craft is a knowledge unknown to the many;

Combination is strength, and unity deifies units.

She will be greatest of great, who makes of a sisterhood sisters.

Milk-white, tinted with rose, as a Being just fresh from the angels,

Beaming in beautiful hope, Basilissa reviv'd from her sickness.

Day is more brilliant than day, just after the dark of a storm-show'r.

Night is more brilliant than night, when Luna pierceth her cloud-veil.

Gold is the brightest of gold, when first cast forth of the furnace.

Life is better than life, when a new-life is born of an old-life.

Chang'd, for the prose of day, was the parable-poem of star-land ;
Type to antitype turn'd, very much as fever to cool blood.

Visions are sent to the wise, and interpretation is wisdom.
Read but the star-book aright and you read to your ultimate profit.
Read Basilissa by light the dream of the parable-garden ;
Much did she learn therefrom, of a possible future for woman.
Much of the force of force, the hidden power of attraction.
Once a queen, and always a queen, though but queenly in dream-land.

Memory lent her aid, that artist original pictures
Copying vividly true, retouch'd by the brush of reflection.
All the star-scene pass'd by ; the heat, the redness, the flowers ;
Lips so ardent with thirst ; dispositions frivolous, lazy ;
Waiters on chance ; idlesse ; and selves most selfishly helpless—
Is there no thirst among girls, no basking and lolling in sunshine,
Biting of tongues for pain, the pain of ungratified cravings ?
Dress is a goddess of morn ; there are infidels to her at noon-day ;
Souls have been sold for clothes, that were flung away ere the soiling ;
Time is when tinsel and rags are as naught, as are jewels and metals ;

One drop of water is more, one drop from the fountain external
More than the precious stones or the purple dyes of Arabia.
Then the attempts of the fair, the futile attempts of the dark one—
Lastly the union of hands, her sole will vincent by union.
Thus revolving the terms, her premisses sought a conclusion,
One link alone in the chain of ocular evidence missing.

What meant the fountain of water all limpid, cool, and refreshing ?

Long she ponder'd this doubt, till she dreamed again from the thinking,
And in her dream she learnt a secret, the lever to work with,
Craft-like, combining her sex in a mystic sisterhood, snapping
Sharp the ferreous chains that have bound them prisoners ever,
Close in the pleasaunce of man, athirst for the waters of freedom.

Secrets are gold in themselves, and givers of gold to their holders.
Tell-tales are spendthrifts who spend in one mad utterance millions.

There is that cannot be told, not e'en by talebearing gossip,
Feeble, malicious, insane, suicidal, religious, or moral.

There is that fears not the slime of the tongue of a venomous serpent.
"Shatter the orb to its fall, the ruins will smite it impavid."

There is that sprung from one seed disperseth itself o'er an acre,
Quiet grower in quiet escaping the harrow by quiet.
Not as the poppy inviter of death by its impudent colour.
Many are gotten of one ; there never was barren conviction ;
Faith communicates faith, as error multiplies error.

Quick the fire was a blaze—a fire that crackled in secret.
She of a nameless creed by no means the fameless avatar.
She, Basilissa, the starr'd, implicit believer in star-light,
Fatalist, following fame, by fame to be Amaranth's equal,
And as his equal his own, was not this his promise in writing ?

Never beholding his face, she still believ'd in his promise.
Men do not lie to their loves ! Are not truth and beauty co-equal ?
Reason forgets to weigh fair words in the balance with motives.

Work that is hopeful is sweet, as sweet is hope to the worker.

Until that day when Amaranth came Basilissa had labour'd
Music entranced.   Then Love eclips'd her radiance of music ;
Wild-love, and wind-love, and cloud-love, tempestuous wreck-love.
Now she began work again, but not on art—her religion,
Rather on woman the soft, inquisitive, pliable, faith-fond ;
Sisters there were not to her, she rather consider'd them school-girls ;
She the Mistress of arts, their warden exacting obedience,
Woman of women to rule in her thorough despising of woman.

   Forms can photograph—forms on the eye leave a positive imprint ;
Dead or alive, on her eye was the form of Amaranth printed,
Seen in the light, under-heard in song, and felt in the darkness ;
Omnipresent—alas ! in all save presence of being.

   Soon gather'd round her fair, and dark ; the serious, merry,
Naughty and proper, and nice, and its nameless reverse of ill-savour,
Noble, and gentle, intelligent, stupid, dumb, and melodious ;
Mostly the richer—the poor have no secret to care for but money,
No ambition but bread ; no higher romance than a surfeit.
Need is a pestle of souls—of weaker souls most completely.

Therefore the great came to court—the court of the queen Basilissa ;
Nor empty-handed—replete with luxurious stores of abundance ;
Diamonds, silks, and furs, bijouterie, bric-a-brac, jewels,
Readily giv'n for a cause, in aid of this sisterhood magic ;
Filling a circle wide, widening, all embracing, expanding ;
Votaries paying their vows ; more than tithing their loveliest caskets,
Much as the houris stripp'd for the rope in the parable-garden.

Mystery, mystic in deed, and far beyond definition,
Imitates things divine, in quality, if not in essence.

Mutterings low all around of a new and marvellous secret,
Fraught by the strangest of girls, transcendently lovely in power ;
Praise commingled with blame ; but many initiate preaching
Loudly the beauty, the force, the truth, of this sisterly bondage,
Knitting a sex in one, which before was self-antagonistic.
Some said she learnt from sound, a system harmonious, perfect ;
Others from colour, of light the primal particles triune ;
Others believ'd the key would be found in some chamber of horrors,
Key to unlock the door—still the door kept fasten'd securely.

Silent, retired, yet firm, Basilissa held her dominion.

Catholic, Protestant, Jew, and the numerous names that are named,

All join'd a nameless creed, supplemental to eldern religions,

Pure in itself as the air, as a garden of roses in spring-time,

Pure as their trysting place, itself a garden of flowers.

Not in the twilight of noon, as the ancient temples of worship,

Sept-colour'd refract of day, interlacing of arches, and circles,

Tracery giving a form to space, geometrical, shapeful,

Seen alone through the veil of golden-canopied saintship,

Polychromatic, as erst the gift-coat of Jacob to Joseph,

Yet translucent, as types of the essence of glorified spirits ;

Colour with shape combin'd, albeit the absence of matter,

Visible through the divine illumination of God's-day,

All-emblematic of hope, of kingdom, victory, triumph,

Painting with flickering hue, the agonis'd face of the Saviour

Bearing his cross—and more—the altar's altar-instruction,

Rhetoric trumpet-ton'd—art-rhetoric, silent, persuasive,

More than Peter the hermit, or Wickliffe, Loyola, Wesley ;

Not in the twilight of noon, as these sacred, venerate temples,

H

Sept-coloured refract of day, the symbols of God's revelation,

But in the æther apert, an æther expressive of freedom,

Natural laws imprint in the heart by a natural conscience,

Common pasture for all—where all may feed in agreement.

Thus—her secret apart—her craft in its energy simple,

Will'd to augment the higher life of higher convictions.

More than this could not be told, except to the secret's betrayal.

This would I never do.   A secret honours the holder,

Asks of the faith of a man protection and confidence, woman.

All in a musical throng, a chord harmonious, vocal,

And in the open air, on turf, quite shaded by leafage

Form'd by a belt of trees, intermix'd with masses of flowers,

Bouquets adorning the bosom of earth, our evergreen mother,

Love-collected, in love they held the lodge of their craftship,

Sweet things to initiate in the sweetest of initiations—

Sensitive, sisterly, fond, almost voluptuous feeling—

One quite unfelt as yet ; a tongue-tying, speechless emotion ;

Raising to higher degrees, more near to the queen Basilissa ;

More near ; for none could approach to her lone supreme exaltation,

Centre star of a system dense revolving around her.

Thus at her zenith of fame, *par angelis, æmula cœli,*

Gain'd she the wish of her heart, the right of Amaranth's promise ;

She was as great as mere fame can make, or unmake a woman,

Follow'd of rank and wealth, best of all acknowledg'd of merit,

Hymn'd by the tattle of girls, admired by men at a distance.

Bodies can fathom a wave, but who knows the depth of the ocean ?

Amaranth dwelt in the wind, and well knew the sound of its blowing ;

Oft had he heard on the breeze a name remember'd for loving,

" Not loved now—oh no !—a buried, hallucinate folly !

" Time is a healer of wounds—ere this she had liv'd down her passion !

" 'Twas but a silly affair, without e'en the merit of evil ;

" Innocent children at play at the very tamest of tame games !

" She was so proper—and he—befool'd by a *fatua ignis.*

" Love is the toy of a boy, a man wants something more solid ;

" Love is a charm to a girl, a woman bursts through such fetters ;

" Twas well no wrong had accrued, by now she had liv'd down her passion."

Metaphysician of lies was Amaranth, son of a Marquis.

Such is the sight of those whose eye-balls are practis'd in squinting !

Look but the wrong way for long, and you'll look the right way for never.

CHORUS.

SISTERHOOD ! Haste, let us haste to crown Basilissa our sister,
   Queen of our garden of love, and queen of the army of women.
Eldest-born of the free, we honour thee, donor of freedom,
Lady ! we bow to thy worth, accept thou the homage of sisters.

Lifter of woman from thrall, thou hast raised thyself to an empire,
Who but the bond can sing aright their deliverer's praises !

Even-song of the stars ! in their many emerald voices,
Part-song in millions of parts, yet each part separate, perfect.

Even-lamps of the sky ! sub-radiant knowledge and power,
Every burner a world, and every world a relation.

Even-dreams in the stars ! when the soul departs from the body,
Flash away to the spheres, an emblem-scenery viewing.

Lesson of love in the stars ! a life the reflex of day-life—

Dream-light, and star-light are one, and both but the shadows of sun-light.

Real is two-parts false—and two-parts mystery real,

Mystic exemplar of death, for death is the truest of all things.

One has revealed free life, we feel it, we see it, we know it,

Each of the essence of each, but she the intensive in essence.

Sisterhood ! haste, let us haste, to crown Basilissa our teacher

Queen of the garden of love, and queen of the army of women !

O sang in praises of her, in a thousand-voic'd adulation

Secret-holders of craft, well-satisfied, enthusiastic,

All advancing in line to crown her the queen of their order.

They had assembled at noon in the garden, their gifts had procur'd her,

Met to enthrone with pomp, with royal garb to invest her—

Boddice of gold, and crimson robes, and necklace of rubies,

Fillet of laurel, and pearls, and priceless diamond chaplet
Set with emerald stars, a constellation of jewels,
And as they came, in groups, they merrily chatted together.

  Bright Basilissa in hope, for she still hop'd in Amaranth's promise,
Beam'd like the sun on a crowd, yet apart she wander'd reflecting
Now on the force of a craft, and now the thoughts of her love-life ;
Dream-life is lovely in sleep, but love-life is best to awake to ;
Fame is a bauble to please, but love is a nugget to covet ;
Hopeful in hope of his love, when on passing a coterie, talking
Girlishly, joyously, fair, intermingled with burstings of laughter,
Heard she an old, old word, a beautiful word of her past life ;
And alas ! join'd with that sound, the hated name of Belinda.
Much astonish'd, she paus'd, transfix'd—but the speaker, unheeding—
Carelessly lilted a line, as a jest to spice up her story ;
" Handsome wedded to plain is a sign of buying and selling ! "
Then as a barb to her dart she mockingly pointed the moral ;
" Amaranth's sold, and Amaranth's bought, and the buyer's Belinda ! "
" Lady Belinda the plain, the wife of Amaranth handsome ! "
Then did the audience jibe in one sough of satirical jibing.

As when the harp in a frost, that instrument warmest of warm sounds,

Most abhorrent of cold, sympathetic, and tuneful, but tender

Sings to the touch the strains of Mendelssohn, Mozart, Beethoven,

Much as to David of old, the inspired precentor of Judah ;

Yet when strain'd by ill-wind it bursts its tune in a second ;

So Basilissa, the wrong'd, the delicate creature of music,

Perfect in temper, in tune far more an artiste than human,

Struck by a sudden chill, the falsehood of Amaranth faithless,

Entering sharp to her soul, as winter a window that's open,

Burst the tune-strings of her heart, and was henceforth voiceless and hollow.

Staggering back to a seat, she sat in vacancy silent.

White was her beautiful face, as the blood ebb'd rapidly heartward,

Victim of lying love, and martyr of innocent trusting.

Even a butcher forbears from the lamb that licks at his fingers—

Who would kill love save love, with his murderous weapon desertion ?

There was a call from one side to the other side of the garden,

" Sisterhood ! gather in one to crown our queen Basilissa !"

Muster'd they wave their hands in the mystical style of their craftship,

And as they slowly advanc'd, they chanted their sisterhood chorus,

Lauding the stars and the dreams, chiefly her the star-led and dreamer,

Founder of woman's craft, the marvellous secret of woman.

One in the front bore the robes, another the necklace and fillet,

Ladies of rank and preferr'd to a higher gradation than others ;

She who was loveliest carried the pearls as a type of complexion ;

She who was sweetest in song the priceless diamond chaplet.

Follow'd the rest in rank, semicircular, closing towards her,

Changing their line to an arch, as they neared the colourless figure.

Shiver'd the wind through the trees, all freezing in spite of the sunshine,

Tremulous shiver'd the wind as they sang in the words of their chorus :

" Sisterhood ! Haste, let us haste, to crown Basilissa our sov'reign,

" Queen of the garden of love, and queen of the army of woman !"

Then the lady who bore on her arm the vesture of crimson

Kneeling obeisance, as one who is honour'd most by obedience,

Crav'd her acceptance of that, the gift of the craftworkers secret.

Silence—and silence—and silence—dead silence, as of dead thing—
No response, but a stare, an horrible stare, and a dull stare,
As from the eyes of one whose soul has escap'd through its eye-balls,
Leaving the pupils fix'd as they were at the moment of leaving.

Whisper'd a little maid, " she is seeing a vision of star-land !"
Answer'd a wiser voice, " she is gone to realisation ! "

Surg'd forth the wave of a cry—the shaking cry of an earthquake,
As they beheld their queen, sitting upright, murder'd, before them—
Dead, they knew not for why ? nor guess'd they the heart-rending reason.
Dead Basilissa had told after all but a part of her secret.
You may make women free of the most celestial craftship,
Be it of stars, or dreams, or sensational, exquisite feeling,
But to be free from love, is not giv'n to man, or to woman.

L'Envoie.

Ladies ! Care ye to know Basilissa's mystical secret ?

OXFORD :
T. AND G. SHRIMPTON,
BROAD-STREET.

www.ingramcontent.com/pod-product-compliance
Lightning Source LLC
Chambersburg PA
CBHW030855260626
47169CB00008B/2546